UNGLUED
THE FIRST TIME TRAVELER
Terry Hayman

Fiero Publishing

Foreword

Hi. Terry Hayman here.

Just wanted to tell you this novella is a prequel to the Jackson Traine series (*Jumpback*, *SCATTER*, and *Fuse* so far). It's certainly readable as a standalone story, but for maximum impact, the best time to read it is right after *SCATTER: Jackson Traine Book Two.* So let's call it Book 2.5 in the series so you can shelve it properly if you're a collector or completist.

And with that, brace yourself for a dive into one of America's less-than-shining moments of history, its documented cruelties captured through my author's imperfect translation and played out by the imagined (though very real to me) characters of my Jackson Traine universe.

Welcome to Iraq in 2003...

October 22, 2003

SALIM

MY NAME IS SALIM Noor al-Rashid.

I write this story in my head to hold on to what is *real* and what is *not.*

In English, because my shame will not let me use the language of my parents.

So...here are my words, spoken in my head, written on an imagined page of paper there to help me capture one fixed set of sensations and events before they shift and change into something else.

Praise Allah!

First, I am 24 years old, unmarried, and strange from birth. I have always been distracted from the ordinary course of life by random sights, smells, sounds, tastes, or feelings that catch my attention so completely I am lost. During Salah, my prayers sometimes sweep me into ecstasy.

When my mother saw this, she prayed I would become an imam. I think she hoped it would help connect me to others, and I would not be so alone.

Instead, shortly after she followed my father to Paradise two years ago, I became a teacher. It made me immensely happy. I understood the innocence of young children, and they understood me.

I also decided *this* year that I would perform Haji, my pilgrimage to the holy city of Mecca, in July. And when I returned, I would ask the parents of my second cousin, Nazya, if she and I could marry.

Yes, I knew Nazya's father, Hafiz, did not approve of my love of American culture (Back Street Boys!!!), nor my lack of family, my times of distraction. But he softened when I joined the Arab Socialist Ba'ath Party under Saddam Hussein to keep my job. It showed I was responsible. Soon I could also say I had embraced all five pillars of Islam—the profession of faith, daily prayers, almsgiving, fasting during Ramadan, and Haji. Hafiz would then most certainly agree to my and Nazya's marriage contract.

These were good plans.

Then the Americans invaded.

Their missiles hit Baghdad before dawn on Friday, March 20th. They shattered buildings and turned the air to fire and smoke around my apartment building, the heat and fumes so intense that I almost swooned, feeling part of them. When I came to myself, I decided they were a sign from Allah that I could not wait for the summer to secure Nazya's hand. I needed to act.

Because there was no school on Fridays and Saturdays, I spent the morning cleaning the dust from my apartment, then dressed in my best clothes and set out to meet with Nazya's father.

When I arrived at their house, however, they had gone. Fled from the city like many others. None of their neighbors knew where they had planned to go.

Perhaps I should have left Baghdad then, chosen a direction, and battled through roadblocks, hunger, and the attacks of others until I found Nazya.

However, I am not so daring. I take *in* the world; I do not shape it.

For this reason, I stayed in Baghdad and continued to teach my students as the Americans bombed, then invaded the city. They destroyed many buildings. We lost our electricity and clean water. But they also helped my conflicted people pull down the big metal statue of Saddam in Firdos Square. Many Iraqis cheered. Saddam had been ruthless. The Iraqis who cheered believed America had so much wealth they would surely share it with us.

This did not happen. At least, not immediately. So my countrymen went crazy with violence. They destroyed government property, killing and looting. They raided armories and distributed weapons and ammunition to insurgent forces. Saddam's old military turned on the Coalition Provisional Authority that the Americans had tried to set up.

Saddam's rule had been brutal but orderly. This was chaos.

By October, shelling and car bombs from insurgents happened every day, the weather grew cold at night, and the Coalition Provisional Authority decided to clean all signs of Saddam's Ba'ath government from Iraq. Since I had become Ba'ath to continue teaching, they fired me.

I now had no money, no electricity, no heat, no students, no friends. But as I walked home in a daze, an old acquaintance stopped me to say he had been traveling up north and seen Nazyah and her family in Aldor.

My heart leaped. *Praise Allah!*

That evening, with a boldness that made me want to call from a minaret like a muezzin, I pulled out of hiding the one thing of value my father had left me—an old Qur'an which he claimed dated back to the Abbasid era. True or not, the book was very old, and I thought its sale might give me enough money to leave Baghdad and find Nazyah.

I stuffed it into my knapsack and rode my bicycle to a heavily bombed neighborhood of southern Baghdad where there was a trader in rare books. I hid my bicycle in an alleyway and ran from one half-destroyed building to another, avoiding places of conflict where American soldiers patrolled in armored vehicles. I was brave! I was a man of conviction!

Until two American soldiers on foot grabbed me.

"Hey! Stop!"

They threw me down on the rubble, and one pinned me there, shoving me over and over against the chunks of broken stones to make me stop screaming while the other searched my backpack. The searcher pulled out my father's gift, saw the age of it, and looked at me with an angry sneer.

"Fucking thief! Terrorist!"

Before I could summon the words to explain, they placed a black hood over my head, bound my wrists behind me, and threw me into a moving vehicle that was louder than any I had ever traveled in. I jolted about until rough hands pulled me up to a seat between others, both men and women, whom I could hear wailing, sniffing, and vomiting. I lost myself in their sorrow.

Until we finally arrived here.

Jahannam, our private hell.

Abu Ghraib prison.

Real.

...

I have been here for two weeks now, I think, in what they call the "Hard Site." This part of the prison is a two-story building of small concrete rooms which have steel bar doors on one side. On my floor, the doors opposite have no bars, just flat steel doors. Total isolation. I hear moans and cries to Allah but see no one except when guards enter to drag me out. The air is thick and stinks always of sweat and garbage, feces and urine. Wild dogs sometimes roam the halls, passing the cells holding "high security" prisoners, those of us supposedly tried and found guilty of terrible crimes.

There are tales that Saddam kept his political prisoners here, hanging scores of them each day.

Now the Americans run it and do even worse.

They torture us daily for information we do not possess. On the advice of other prisoners, I do not let them know I speak English. It makes no difference. They beat us. They shave our beards. They make us go naked and do sexual things while their women watch.

They put us in positions of so much pain we pass out. They take our sleep, take our breath, shackle and drag us, make us crawl in our own—

No!

They try to take everything from us, including Alhamdulillah and the magnification of Allah.

I must not let them go. Yet...for someone who has always had trouble focusing, how can I possibly hold on to anything?

It is why, as I now lie naked on the filthy, wet floor of my cell, I continue this story in my head. Words spoken and written, recalling sights, sounds, feelings, facts. I make a dua to Allah that I may remember them all for what they are.

This.

That.

Myself.

Yet I fear that even as I do this, it may not be enough. For I fear I am becoming *hrayroo-lah'ssuh-quin.*

Unglued.

No!

Review!

Yes.

My name is Salim Noor al-Rashid...

GORDON

OKAY, THIS IS DAY One. Yep! Journaling time, Gordo.

Gotta start with the crazy-shit way this world turns. Take my career. Four months ago, I was an Army MP on my second tour of Iraq, studying Arabic and bucking for a promotion, when I got diagnosed with Crohn's disease. The Army kicked me out—stupid regs!—but I got hired on with Comsee International a couple weeks later. Now I'm back in Iraq in one of the sites most targeted by enemy fire and IEDs.

Abu Ghraib prison. Jesus.

And I'm here as a frigging interrogator.

Because of my language skills, obviously. Also, I have experience in the region, so I know enough not to get myself blown up on an IED by casually ripping out along any of the roads around this place.

Not that I plan to go out much. They've given us cells—yeah, literally concrete block rooms. They got solid doors, and are in a different building from the prisoners in the Hard Site, Tier 1A and Tier 1B, but still. In our rooms/cells, I guess we're going to sleep, read, journal, masturbate, what have you. The CIA guys we flew in with are in a different block, but I doubt their accommodations are much better. Everything here is crumbling cinderblock or crumbling brick and mortar. Places that were painted, like all those halls with gaudy pictures of Saddam-fucking-Hussein, are chipped and painted or defaced. Our troops are repainting some areas, but it's definitely like trying to cover mold. The rot's still there. Inevitably seeps out.

I've been meeting soldiers and intelligence people nonstop since I came in, but the one I want to mention is a head shrink who came in with the CIA guys. Name's Dr. Uwe Bent. That's pronounced Oo-vuh, and he's a bona fide psychiatrist. Originally from Switzerland, I think.

He flew in on the same Hercules I did. And I don't want to sound gay, but the doc's really striking. Tall, long neck, high forehead. A touch of gray in the temples, though he looks like he's not even 40. He's also got these amazing, sparkling blue eyes.

I couldn't help staring at him during our take-off and finally got his name and background from the Comsee commander strapped in beside me on the line of web seats that lined each side of the hold. I changed webbed seats once we'd reached altitude and plopped down beside Bent, strapping in just as the plane started to rock and roll through a patch of turbulence, the props roaring even louder than usual.

I asked Bent, almost shouting, why he was coming all the way out to Abu Ghraib.

"Why do you think?" he called back.

"Because you're a good interrogator?"

He seemed to think that was funny. "Perhaps. But I believe that's why the government hired you people, isn't it? What is your name?"

"Gordon Trench, sir."

"Ditch digger in a former life?"

"Not that I know of, sir."

"It would explain your need to come out here in this one. Do you have a degree in psychology, Gordon?"

"No. I was Military Police."

"Ah. A young man's game."

"I guess."

"You're sorry you left it. Heart condition? No. Schizophrenia? No. Bowel problems? Ah. Better than discovering you'd developed Lyme disease or epilepsy, I suppose."

The fact he'd read me so fast pissed me off, but I laughed. "Ha. You're good. But if you're not here to help with interrogating the prisoners..."

"I'm here to study. Observe. Make...suggestions."

The way he said it made me shiver and stop asking questions. Everything else had been relaxed and professional, if a bit pompous. But that last thing? It made me feel like a mouse in a maze, with Dr. Bent fascinated to see which way I'd run.

Anyway...

That was two days ago. We arrived late. All of today was orientation, and I didn't see Bent at all. Sun's down now. The heat's dropped enough that I might be able to sleep. First rounds tomorrow.

2

October 23, 2003 – A

SALIM

!

I startle awake.

It is not because the guards want me to. Those times, they use loud music and bright lights, sometimes strobe lights. It makes me lose track of time and who I am.

This is something else.

What woke me is a sound from the neighboring cell block where they lock up the wives, sons, and daughters of prisoners on our block to use against us. Some of us. The sound is a panicked scream in the darkness. Then more. A young woman's sound. Maybe a girl. Someone's wife or daughter is being attacked and raped by a guard or an interrogator. Or perhaps it is by an Iraqi civilian who is friends with the night guards.

It has become a familiar sound since I have come here. It gives much perspective to the crude labels one of the female guards likes to write on our bodies. Last week she wrote "RAPEIST" (her spelling) on the leg of a prisoner I did not know.

Perhaps they do not consider it rape if the woman is an Iraqi prisoner.

Just as they do not consider it torture or an abomination, what they do to me and my fellows.

Allah, protect your people, all your children. *Allahu Akbar!*

I am becoming unglued.

My naf, my being, wants to fly away, become one with the madness more than I normally do, and end myself.

But Allah calls us to listen to him. To live in his way.

Therefore, I will fight both my nature and my torture to hang onto myself.

I will make this world real with repetition and thereby make myself real.

I breathe and write it again in my head.

!

I startle awake....

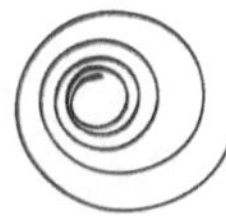

GORDON

Time?

Past midnight.

Can't sleep.

I thought I heard a girl screaming. Maybe that's what woke me. Or maybe it was another round of mortar shells hitting nearby. I swear, if the insurgents had Tomahawks, they'd have blown this place up months ago. They would have counted the loss of Iraqi prisoners a necessary sacrifice.

Maybe I'm just awake because I don't know what I'm going to find on my rounds tomorrow. I've heard rumors.

I think I'll start with Camps Ganci and Vigilant tomorrow, where they hold the people who were mostly wrong-place, wrong-time. Then wander way out to Camp Redemption, where they hold detainees who may or may not be guilty of something. Finally, if I have time, I'll go to the hard sites, Tiers 1A and 1B. Probably won't have time for the hard sites tomorrow. Probably won't.

Good. I can sleep on that.

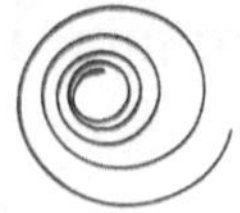

SALIM

AGAIN, I STARTLE AWAKE. This time is because someone kicked me with a boot.

They do so again.

I squint because a bright light is shining into my eyes. It is another trick they use, I think, to make us lose track of time. Is it morning? Afternoon? Still the middle of the night? I may have slept one hour or four or twelve.

Write this down! Remember!

Yes.

I write in my head that my mind spins, and every part of my body hurts from sleeping naked on the concrete floor, but I can feel each part of my skin suck at the still-wet pieces of concrete, glued to it as much as to my naf. A bruise on my head throbs. Was that from me banging it against the cinder-block wall this night or from some beating yesterday? Earlier today?

I wrinkle my nose back at the sharp, rancid smell coming from the sticky concrete under me. I have peed myself in my sleep, though I do not remember when this happened. My groin has been so often attacked by sticks that I no longer have clear sensation down there nor control of my urination.

"Git up, ya little sand nigger!"

His exact words.

Remember them!

I write that he is a pale pink, hulking monster above me. Brown camo pants with metal handcuffs dangling from one pocket. Olive tee-shirt. Mustache. I have seen this man many times before. He is cruel. The sight makes me mutter a prayer to Allah. This earns me another kick to my ribs, then the monster's fleshy hand reaches down, grabs one of my ears, and drags it upwards as my feet struggle to get themselves under me and follow my it up.

"C'mon, Akbar. Move it!"

I fight harder to steady myself and stay on my feet after the monster releases my ear.

This is when I see there is a second man in the cell, standing just behind the hulking monster's shoulder. He is light brown and smaller, like me. Iraqi. He must be an interpreter because he is dressed like an American soldier—full battle dress, including the boots, but no body armor or helmet. Maybe he left those outside. He has greasy hair, but it is cleaner than mine. I guess his usual job is working with American soldiers in the danger zones around Baghdad. Coming in here is what he does on his time off.

He waves at me with a big smile, then says to my guard, "Let me speak to him."

The mustached monster grunts and steps back.

The interpreter steps very close to me, then backs away a little, his nose wrinkling back. He says in Arabic, "He wants you to go with him to be interrogated."

I stare at him blankly, marveling that this traitor to his people thinks his ability to speak both Arabic and English should entitle him to the friendship of America. Then he repeats his information in Kurdish and what I think is Turkmen. He is more gifted in languages than I thought.

"I don't speak Turkmen," I say quietly in Arabic.

"Ah. Neither did the girl next door," the interpreter says, reverting happily back to my tongue. He points to where I heard the sounds of rape last night. "I fucked her anyway. I have privileges here."

I stare at him, shocked.

"Don't look at me like that." He slips back into Arabic to say, "It means I can help you. You are going to see a powerful American today. When they bring you back here, I am going to come here again. You will tell me about him. If you help get me what I want, I will help you get free."

This sets my mind on fire, but before I can respond, the pink-skinned monster spits on the floor and says, "Taking too long, Benny."

I see the interpreter react to what must be his name. He steps back. Suddenly, the guard pulls a foul-smelling black sack over my head. I hear the clink as he pulls the handcuffs from his pocket, then he ratchets one on my wrist, pulls it behind my back, and traps my other wrist there, too. He shoves me to get me walking blindly forward.

More disorientation.

Remember!

I'm trying!

Like the time tricks and beatings, I believe the hoods are supposed to make me answer questions. But the questions are always about things I do not know, and I think the guards know this. For them, it is really about punishment. They want revenge on us for not bowing whenever they approach, for not kissing their boots, for not praising their god, for making them come to our country to secure their oil supplies. It is not what they say, but it is what I believe.

As I walk, the monster hits me again, spits on the back of my head, and I feel myself crumble inside. There is no "us" anymore. There is just me, in a swirling void of pain and fear, that more and more I find myself pushing away, the world with it. My bare feet shuffle across gritty floors. My head bounces softly, unable to remain high and proud.

I have lost all pride. In myself. In Allah. In life.

Remember?

The pink monster behind me pokes me to make me turn the corner and enter a room I cannot see, but which feels different somehow from others I have entered in this *Jahannam*. It is cooler. The floor is smoother. The air presses into me like I have entered an airtight freezer. Above all, even through my foul hood, I can hear, smell, and sense the presence of someone new. The powerful American? It is as if his focus on me is a spotlight that burns my blood inside me.

I make myself straighten. I will pretend I am a man. I will remember all of this for my dead parents, for Nazyah, and for myself, so I have something to pass back to Benny. For if there is any hope that I can get free of this place, I will take it. Even if it means dealing with a hundred devils.

The hood is ripped up off my head.

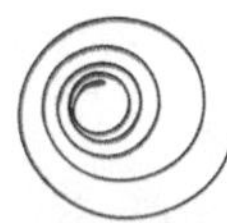

GORDON

Jesus. What a crap day. My first interrogation and I fucking kill the prisoner.

Here's how it happened.

Some orderly rousted me off my crappy little cot and mattress at 4-fucking-a.m. and told me I had to show up at Room Delta in Tier 1A. And here I thought I outranked all the stupid MPs now that I worked for a private contractor. I didn't answer to these guys. Maybe to the female general in charge of this prison, but I didn't think it was her ordering me up.

So who? The CIA guys? I doubted it. They were smart, but lazy bastards.

That was when I figured it had to be Dr. Bent, Mr. creepy *"I'm here to study. Observe. Make...suggestions."*

On my way to Room Delta, really missing my morning coffee, I thought up some pretty pointed suggestions for *him.*

Then I arrived, pushed my way in through the steel door labeled Delta, and my grumpy bravado nosedived into sour bile.

It was Bent, like I thought. He sat like Saint Peter, except at the gates of Hell, not Heaven, in a folding steel chair on the far side of this cement box of a room. He was off to one side, though, and half-hidden behind a table that held a pile of rags, a clipboard with a pen and some papers, a couple plastic glasses, a jug of water. Maybe he *was* there just to study after all? Not judge. Not run things.

To his right, in the middle of the wall, someone had hoisted a stripped steel bedframe up on its end and leaned it back against the wall, metal legs sticking outwards like it was some kind of overturned cockroach. Bolted there?

Dead center in the room, meanwhile, were two men I hadn't seen before.

The first was a jaunty-looking (for 4-fucking-a.m.) guard with brown hair, brown mustache, dressed in summer camo pants and olive tee-shirt. In front of him, on his knees like he'd just been shoved down, was a skinny Iraqi man. The Iraqi looked maybe thirty but could have been as young as twenty. With the stubble, ragged hair, slack jaw, haunted eyes, and scrapes and filth over most of his body, it was hard to tell. He'd somehow tucked his penis down between his legs in a hopeless attempt at modesty. His hands were cuffed behind his back.

Fuck. I knew it. I knew this was what I was getting into. I'd heard the rumors. Knew it even before then, I think, after Comsee made us read the DOJ's and DoD's memos that essentially exempted interrogation from torture restrictions in a time of war when you needed info for self-defense.

"Where are his clothes?" I said.

"They're killers and scum," said the guard with a bit of a midwestern crunch. "Don't deserve clothes."

"Really? Where's his file? What was he picked up for?"

The guard's sneer sagged a little. "Carrying stolen goods. Plotting with terrorists."

"You've confirmed that?"

"Now that you're finally here, we will. Right?" The guard slapped the back of the Iraqi's head, almost making the man tumble forward. "We softened him up like they told us. Happy to hang him from the rack there, if you need." He gestured to the upended steel bedframe. Definitely bolted to the wall then. Used as a rack of sorts. How creative...if you were a sadist.

"What's your name?"

"Specialist Devers. Sir!" The guard said it like he expected a reward for his initiative.

"Not going to happen, Devers," I said.

He shrugged but still looked eager. Like maybe he was going to salivate on the stone floor or stroke himself inside his pants.

"You can go," I said.

The guard's eyebrows shot up. "Doc?" he said to Bent. "I'm s'posed to stay here and guard him."

Bent just redirects the guard's gaze to me.

"You can shut the door and lock it," I said. "We'll bang when we're done."

The guard stared at me, then at Bent. Finally, accepting his early morning entertainment had vanished on him, the guard shook his head in disgust and backed out, shutting and locking the door behind him.

I waited a beat, then walked over and kicked the metal door in case the guard had his ear to it. Thought I heard a vague, "Ow!"

When I turned back to the center of the room, Bent said, "Was that because you worried he'd report you went too rough on this detainee or too easy?"

It didn't sound like a judgment or a warning. More like curiosity about whether I was a sadist, sap, or professional. I wasn't sure of that myself yet. Just knew I was pissed. "Did they give you a file? His name? Anything?"

Bent smiled thinly and reached for the clipboard on the table in front of him. He lifted it and held it up toward me. I walked past the prisoner, who hadn't said boo since I'd entered. Hadn't even grunted when he got slapped on the back of his head. Just stayed on his knees, naked, hands cuffed behind his back, dull eyes staring forward and down before him.

I took the clipboard from Bent and read it.

No picture of the prisoner. Just some typed notes. The time and place they'd picked him up, the item they believed he'd stolen, and a vague reference to shouted Arabic phrases associated with other terrorists they'd caught planting bombs near American depots and vehicles. Arabic phrases? Like what? *Allahu Akbar?* Nothing like freaking out over someone praising their god in a language you didn't get.

Also, a name: Salim Noor al-Rashid.

I wondered how they'd gotten that from him. Had he been carrying ID? Or was that the one thing they'd asked him that he'd known the answer to?

I handed the clipboard back to Dr. Bent and turned to the prisoner.

"So, Salim. That your name?"

The prisoner didn't raise his head or answer.

I looked at Bent. "Do we even know if he speaks English?"

Bent shrugged.

"Do we have a local translator handy?"

The prisoner's head shot up, and his gaze met mine directly, totally focused. I couldn't quite read the expression on the man's face, though. Fear? Disgust?

"You speak some English, then," I said. "Good. You've clearly been beaten, stripped, maybe other things. I can stop all that right now. Long as you tell us what you know."

Al-Rashid's face dropped again. His shoulders sagged.

"Yeah, I know," I said, walking around him, noting the bruises, cuts, and scrapes, none properly healed. Some looked infected. The info sheet said he'd been brought in on the seventh. I wondered if all this stuff had happened since then or... "Salim, were you part of a gang or a group of people trying to blow things up?"

He didn't answer verbally but shook his head like his body couldn't help denying it. Not very convincing.

"You run messages for people? Plan things with them? To get the Americans out of Baghdad, maybe?"

Al-Rashid twitched and started muttering at the floor. It sounded like, "Buh...buh...buh...."

"You do?" I pressed.

He just kept muttering at the floor. "Buh...buh...."

"You need to motivate him, Gordon," said Dr. Bent from his chair. "Do you need suggestions?"

I shot a nasty look at Bent. I'd been a fucking MP in this country not two months ago, disciplining both our troops and theirs, sometimes their civilians. I knew how to "motivate" someone. I just wasn't sure this situation called for it. Not yet.

"You could start with the handcuffs," said Bent. "Just lift them. A small thing."

It *was* a small thing, so I did it. I grabbed the center of the cuffs that bound Al-Rashid's wrists behind him and lifted.

Al-Rashid screamed and his head twisted to look me in the eye again. This time I could read it. Betrayal. Sliding into...hate.

"My...one...de...*sigh*...er!" he barked at me with a heavy accent, almost spitting.

"Is to do what?" I barked back at him, still holding his wrists up behind him, high enough that his shoulders started quaking and trying to twist away from the pain. "You want to hurt me? Fight back?"

"Buh! Buh! Back street!" he barked at me.

"I'm sure you'd rather have met me there than here, right?" I yanked his wrists back and forth so he screamed again. Amazing how much pain you can cause by pulling joints in unnatural directions.

But rather than spitting at me again, the guy started mumbling in Arabic, his eyes fluttering, his voice cracking and whispering and rolling through what I was pretty sure was one of their damn ritual sequences of glorifying Allah, asking forgiveness for their sins, or asking for help for every damn little thing you can think of.

And fucking damn if his face wasn't goddamned glowing with a transported kind of trance happiness.

Well, that wasn't happening on my watch, during my first ever interrogation in this prison, with Dr. Uwe Bent recording everything, probably to report back to my Comsee bosses and get me yanked from what could be my last chance of making a career for myself over here. Two strikes yer out!

I dropped to my knees in front of Salim and grabbed his jabbering face with both my hands. "Hey, Salim!" I yelled at him to no effect as he jabbered on, eyes almost rolling back in his head.

I slapped him so hard across the face that it spun the small man sideways away from me.

In slow motion, I saw his head arcing half over his bent knees as his wrists jerked free of my left hand. Then his head plunged towards the concrete floor like a hairy melon and hit it with a *SMACK!*

3

October 23, 2003 – B

SALIM

A BRIGHT LIGHT IS shining into my eyes, and my mind is racing.

What? Where?

Is this real?

I was recording my thoughts and experiences in an empty cement room with a metal door. A cold, frightening American was there when the guard brought me in. Then a younger American more my age entered. He was so much like me, I could almost read his thoughts.

He did not want to be there. Like me.

He felt lost, not sure of his purpose in this place. Like me.

Alone and bullied to comply. Like me.

This happened. I wrote it. I saw, smelled, felt, heard, and wrote it in my mind.

Real.

I wrote that the younger American started to lose his patience with the room and me. He shouted questions at me. He did not listen when I tried to answer him, to tell him I loved America, at least the Backstreet Boys. And I prayed for him (and myself) so loudly it felt like I was yelling. Or the room was yelling, for it brought me again into a state of ecstasy.

Real!

And then he hit me and....

I am here.

A boot kicks me for what I sense is the second time. Familiar. Because it is also familiar that I am lying face down, naked, on sticky concrete, and the smell of stale urine rises around me so strongly I want to gag. Except that I have no moisture in my mouth, just as I have no sensation in my groin as I try to sit up.

"Git up, ya little sand nigger!"

That was exactly what he said the...last time?

When I look at the pink-skinned guard above me, he looks the same as I remember him from that time as well. Hours ago? Days? He wears brown camo pants with metal handcuffs trailing from one pocket. Olive tee-shirt. Mustache. His name is Specialist Devers. I start to mutter a prayer to Allah but remember it made him kick me before, so I freeze my tongue.

I have been too slow, and the guard bends down to grab one of my ears and drag it upward. I duck his hand and scramble to my feet. There I weave about, my head is spinning with confusion.

"Okay, Akbar...."

I know somehow, feel somehow, that this is not *like* before. It *is* before. All of this.

For this reason, it is not a surprise when I turn to see the other man who was here before, my greasy-haired compatriot, in his full American battle dress. The rapist. He is about to open his mouth when I blurt in Arabic, "I have met you!"

It shocks him into silence for a moment. Then he turns to the pink-skinned guard and says, "He is confused. I will tell him why he needs to go with you."

He turns back to me. "Now...."

Again in Arabic, I babble, "You fucked a young woman last night here in the hard site. You speak Arabic, English, Kurdish, and Turkmen. I am to be taken before an important American, and you want me to tell you about him. If I do, you will help me escape this place."

He wrinkles his nose at my stink and takes a step back from me. I wobble in my starved, beaten, barely awake body.

The guard grabs the interpreter's arm. "What's he saying?"

He lies, "That he is hungry and cold and wants food."

"There are *two* Americans waiting to question me," I mutter at him in Arabic. "One is a doctor." I finally remember the interpreter's name. "Please, Benny."

The guard, Devers, shoves the interpreter from him. "You're fucking lying to me. He said, 'Am-ree-kee-on.' And your name. You plotting with him, Benny? You trine to get us blown up?"

"No, no, my friend," says Benny, suddenly very scared and backing away. "No."

Because Benny may be my only escape, I try to save him by calling out, "Devers!"

The guard whirls on me. "Wha'd you say?"

"Specialist Devers is your name."

The guard's face lights up like a man in heat. "And here we din't know you even spoke English! Alright then. This's gonna be fun!"

And again, he pulls out the stinking hood from somewhere and puts it over my head. He yanks my hands behind me and handcuffs my wrists together. He pushes me so hard that I stumble against a hard wall, hitting my head.

"Oops!" says Devers' loud voice before he laughs, grabs my shoulder, and redirects me.

Soon I can feel we are out in the main space between the cells of misery. I can hear the other prisoners, the ones who are awake, quietly sobbing or gasping to breathe, to survive.

And I try to plan how I will reach the American who is like me before he becomes lost in his anger....

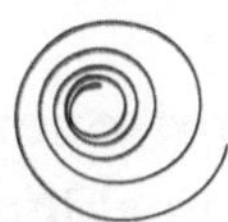

GORDON

BY THE TIME I pushed my way in through the steel door labeled Delta, I was sinking into a sour state of resentment that just got worse when I saw Bent waiting for me.

He was sitting on the far side of this sweat-box of a concrete room, looking all cool and judgey. He was up against the far wall, off-center, behind a table that held rags, a clipboard, some glasses, a jug of water. Observing, I guessed. Not doing the actual work.

But what the hell was an upended bedframe doing against the middle of the wall beside him?

Didn't matter. In the middle of the room was the work. Two men there I hadn't seen before.

The first was a mustached guard looking way too happy for 4 a.m. Bit of an asshole grin on his face.

The other man was obviously a prisoner, naked and kneeling by the guard's legs, his hands cuffed behind his back. The prisoner was Iraqi, of course, his light brown skin looking bruised, ripped, and generally ill-used. His hair and beginnings of a beard looked like they had never been washed. He'd tucked his penis down between his legs, either in modesty or a hopeless attempt to protect them from further abuse.

Like what the fuck were we all doing in this place? I mean, I knew the restrictions on torture had effectively been lifted for this war, but this? Looked more like someone had just been acting out on this guy.

"Where are his clothes?" I said.

"They're killers and scum," said the guard. "They don't—"

"That is not true," said the prisoner.

Yeah. Right on top of the guard's speech. Without even lifting his head. I'm not sure he had the strength to lift his head.

"You speak English," I said.

The guard whapped the prisoner on the back of his head, almost knocking him down. "Fucking turd don't—"

"Shut up!" I snapped at him.

He literally took a step backward, staring at me with his mouth hanging open.

"Get out," I ordered him.

"S'posed to guard him," he said, waving a finger at the prisoner.

I bared my teeth. "Get out. I'll come get you when we're done."

The guard left, almost tripping over himself as he went out and slammed the steel door after him.

"Salim Noor al-Rashid," said Bent from behind his little table. I saw he was reading from the clipboard. "Caught thirteen days ago trying to smuggle a stolen book to terrorists south of Baghdad. Screamed out some terrorist phrases."

"Like?" I said.

"Doesn't say."

"It is a lie," whispered the prisoner.

"Another one?" I said.

The prisoner, Al-Rashid, was now looking up at me. And over at Bent. His right eye was all bloodshot like he'd been punched there or it was infected. For some reason, that set off a growing panic in me. Like they'd say I beat him up. Or that I *would* beat him up.

"You must know this is a lie, doctor," the man said to Bent in the tiniest, most pathetic, all Iraqi simper.

"Hey," I snapped. "Talk to me. I'm the one in charge here."

"Why do you think I'm a doctor?" Bent asked.

"Specialist Devers called you Doc," whimpered al-Rashid, then looked at me with his bloodshot eye. "You called this man Gordon. And I am..." He trailed off a minute, gagging on something, then gasping like the guard's last kick had made it hard to breathe. "I am Salim."

I shoved my hand through my hair. "That the name of the guard brought you in? Devers?" Any control I'd had felt like it was slipping away while my early morning pre-coffee headache pounded louder by the minute. From the dry air, maybe. Or all the crumbling mold in this place.

Al-Rashid said nothing.

"I *asked* you a question!"

"Actually," said Bent, without rising from his chair. "I have a different question. Do you read minds, Salim?"

Al-Rashid blinked at him, his face jerking in terror.

"Because I never called this man Gordon. And I'm betting that Specialist Devers never called me Doc before coming into this room. He certainly didn't call me that after you and he entered."

"So you're taking over the interrogation?" I asked.

Bent shrugged. "Just a question."

"Well, I have a better question. *Questions.*" I strode right up in front of Al-Rashid and dropped to a squat in front of him. "You tell me, Salim, who you were going to give the book to."

"I was going to sell it. It was from my father, and he said—"

"Is that who you stole it from?" I snaked out a hand and slapped him across his face. I wasn't even sure why. Not sure I cared.

"He left it with me when—"

I slapped him again.

Salim's eyes brimmed with tears, and he looked at the floor. "Now, doctor, you tell him to lift my handcuffs. A small thing. 'Motivation.'"

"Fuck!" I slapped him again, reached over his back, and grabbed the cuffs. I stood up, hoisting his arms above his head as I did so, making the silly haji scream so loud it hurt my ears.

"Salim!" Dr. Bent boomed out like he was suddenly trying to be Shakespearean. "You tell me, *Mary had a little lamb. Its fleece was white as snow!* Remember that!"

It was enough to drive me a little mad, I think, because I jerked Salim's arms higher then higher again, all my strength, until something went *SNAP!*

4

October 23, 2003 – C

SALIM

THE SCREAMS.

My screams? No, they are not. They are the screams of a young woman. A girl, maybe.

And my arms!

I move them where I lie face down on the cold concrete in the black stink of my cell. They are stiff and sore like most of my body, every cut and bruise moaning at me. But my arms and shoulders are whole. Not snapped. Not separated. Not whatever I remember feeling as Gordon gave in to the evil of this place and tried to hurt me more than the hurt he felt inside.

That was real.

Is this real, too?

This is real.

The girl screams again, and I force myself to push against the floor until I can bring one knee up under me. Then another.

Her scream is so much worse than the sound of dying. It is the sound of violation, of the world turning upon her, of Allah leaving her to al-Aduw, the Enemy.

It terrifies me.

With all the strength still in me, I push myself up to my feet. I waver and almost fall but do not. Instead, I stumble to the bars of my cell in the darkness, one feeble light down the hall giving vague shape to the two floors of cells housing Iraqi prisoners like me.

How many are awake in the dark now, listening to the screams?

Is there one among them who knows that cry as their wife? Their daughter?

My fingers wrap around the pitted steel of my cell bars, and I try to shake them but shake only myself. Still, I yell with more voice than I could have imagined, "Stop! Stop! Stop!" In Arabic, because I know who is making the girl scream. If I could yell in Turkmen, I would.

Amazingly, impossibly, I am heard.

The sounds of the girl's screaming stop. There are sounds of metal doors clanging. Things thump. A door in our building slams open, and boots pound the ground.

I let myself stumble back and fall to the ground where I was before, going still like I am dead. I feel dead. I will be dead if they know it was me who yelled.

The boots tromp down our corridor between cells, and a beam of light shines into my cell. Through slitted eyes, I see it pan across the floor and stop on top of me, then move on. The boots move on as well.

I continue to lie still, naked in the muck of my urine-flavored sweat. Unable to move. My mind spins.

Is this really the night before?

Must I meet Benny, Specialist Devers, Gordon, and the doctor all over again?

Was my time in the hell not long enough already?

Or...has Allah given me an answer to my secret dua, my prayer that my time here means something, or that He will deliver me? Is this a power of knowledge? Of having the chance to try different things? To yell rather than stay silent?

The cold cement under my cheek says no.

The quiet where once a girl screamed says...maybe?

Allah, give me strength. *Allahu Akbar!*

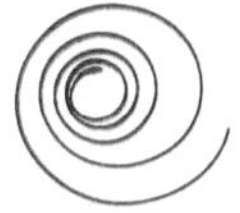

GORDON

PAST MIDNIGHT.

Can't sleep. Write it out.

First rounds tomorrow, and my stomach's in knots. Got a bad feeling about this whole venture.

Maybe because I woke up to the sound of a girl screaming somewhere like she was dying. But by the time I was fully awake and out of my bed, there was shouting and the screams stopped.

It was all distant, though I'm pretty sure it came from the Hard Site, Tiers One and Two. That's what all the rumors are about, those two places. Whispers about them even on the plane flying out here. Then the whisperer would catch my eye and fall silent. Wasn't sure if that was because they knew I was going to be going in there and didn't want to scare me, or because the fact I was going already tainted me. Like I was going to be part of it.

They didn't take us into the Hard Site on our first day's orientation. Was that why? Delaying our transformation?

Screw it. I'm not Army anymore. I'm private sector. Don't have to follow orders like a robot. I'll assess. Do my job. Do what's *right*.

I have that power.

Good. I can sleep on that.

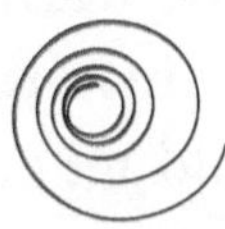

SALIM

I AM AWAKE AFTER the first kick, scrambling to my feet even as Specialist Devers tries to shine a bright light into my eye.

His self-satisfied face looks surprised I could move so quickly after the way the guards assaulted me the day before and threw me down to sleep naked on the concrete floor.

Indeed, many places of my body throb with pain, but they seem distant from me. As if, in the way I did with my injured groin, I have withdrawn my residence in them so they cannot hurt me further. This began, I realize, the day the two American soldiers assaulted me and brought me here, and it has grown worse each day.

A piece of me warns that if I do not reconnect, I will become fully unglued. This is maybe why I am jumping in time as well.

"Got up fast, sand nigger," says the guard. "Like maybe you know what's coming, hunh?"

He makes a fake lunge at me with his fist. When I only blink at him, he slaps me hard across the face. Then he waits for some sign of defiance so he can slap me again.

But I am not looking at him. I am watching Benny, who has finally entered the cell behind Devers.

"Let me speak to him," Benny says. He steps close, and Specialist Devers steps back.

Before Benny can say another word, though, I speak to him quickly in Arabic. "I am going to see an interrogator named Gordon and a doctor. What do you want from them?"

"What do you mean?" he asks in our language that Devers cannot follow.

I pause. How can I tell him I know this? Lying is haram, a forbidden sin. Finally, I say the truth in this way: "I had a vision of meeting you. You spoke to me in Kurdish and Turkmen as well as Arabic, and told me I would meet someone important today. You said if I told you about them, you might help me escape this place."

"What's he yakkin' about?" Devers says.

Benny looks at me oddly. Then he turns with a serious face toward Devers. "He says he is faint with hunger and pain. He is not sure he will be able to hold back the truth before those who question him today."

"Ha. You're so full of shit. Move!"

Devers shoves Benny to one side and produces the foul-smelling hood he puts over my head. As he yanks me around to handcuff my hands behind my back, Benny says in fast Arabic, "I want to leave this country. Get me attached to someone who can take me out with them, and I will help you."

Then I am shoved from my cell, blind and disoriented, stumbling along on legs and feet I barely know.

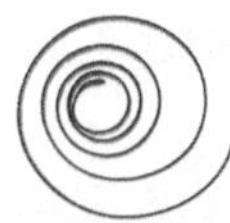

GORDON

SO THIS IS WHAT I fucking *thought* was going to happen. Bent taking over. Me consigned to some bullshit support role. And I'm still going to get blamed for the way this all went FUBAR.

Do my job? Do what's right?

By the time I came limping into my first Tier1 interrogation assignment, in a concrete box-of-a-room labeled Delta, Dr. Uwe Bent was already there, sitting behind a little table along the back wall like some kind of judge. He had a clipboard and pen, obviously ready to take notes and assess my performance. The upturned bedframe bolted to the wall beside him was instantly recognizable as some kind of torture device, too. Probably to stretch out anyone who didn't pass muster.

Fuck.

My head was already pounding from being woken up at 4 a.m. and rousted out here with no coffee. I thought the point of that kind of shit was to disorient the prisoners, not the interrogators.

Speaking of which....

After I banged my way in, saw Bent, and died a little inside, I took in the mustached guard and the naked, beaten-up looking prisoner—excuse me, *detainee*—who was kneeling just in front of him. Both were in the center of the mostly bare room like they knew they were the center of attention, the reason for everyone being here.

The guard looked so fucking smug.

"Why's he naked?" I asked him.

"They're killers and scum," said the guard. "Don't deserve clothes."

"Really? Where's his file? What was he picked up for?"

"Carrying stolen goods. Plotting with terrorists."

"You've confirmed that?"

"Now that you're here, we will. Right?"

"Get out of here!"

The guard stuck out his lower jaw. "I'm s'posed to guard him."

"So lock the door behind you. We'll bang and yell when we're done. Seems to be the only thing that gets people's attention around here in the middle of the goddamn fucking night when there are rapes going on!"

The guard frowned at me but seemed to get the point and hurried out, closing the door behind him. There was a grating sound that suggested he'd actually done what I suggested and locked us in.

Wonderful.

I turned toward Bent, still feeling at this point like I had a say in how things proceeded from here. "Is there any kind of file on this detainee?"

Before Bent could answer, the naked prisoner on his knees raised his face to the ceiling and began calling out some loud prayer to Allah. In the Iraqi dialect, you still get the Arabic softening of certain consonants, but it rolls the R's harder and gives more gut-vomit sound to the H's. When I'd been learning it as an MP, the Iraqi teachers had boasted their dialect could make

Arabic speakers in other countries like Lebanon, Syria, or Egypt step back in fear.

Then, like it was just a continuation of the same prayer, the prisoner suddenly switched to strongly accented English with, "Mary had a little lamb! Its fleece was white as snow!"

Bizarre, right? Except you should have seen the reaction of Dr. Bent. The man's face went white, and he stood up so fast he knocked over the small table.

"What?" I said. "So he speaks some English."

Bent ignored me. He walked right up to the prisoner. Stood right in front of him, where I should have been by then. "Salim!" he said. "Look at me!"

Salim?

The naked Iraqi blinked and lowered his face slightly to look at Dr. Bent's face.

Must have been a little like looking into the face of God, given the doc's physical presence, the high, back-combed dark hair, the straight nose, clean jawline, the glittering blue eyes.

"Salim, why did you say what you just said? Mary had a little lamb. Its fleece was white as snow."

Captured by Bent's presence, Salim just blurted it out. "You told me I should say this."

Bent didn't skip a beat. "When did I tell you?"

The Iraqi's dirt-smeared, bruise-covered face screwed up like he either didn't know or didn't want to say. To my surprise, though, he finally spoke. "The last time here."

"But I've never been here before today."

The Iraqi nodded. "Yes. Today."

"In this room with us?"

The Iraqi nodded again.

Bent looked at me with a bemused expression. I returned one that did its best to convey, *What the fuck?* Bent seemed to find that funny.

He looked back to the Iraqi, not inviting the man to stand or even free his penis from where he'd squeezed it down between his thighs when he kneeled. Religious modesty obviously makes you inventive.

"Salim," Bent said, "listen to me very carefully. Do you believe you were at this place with us, then jumped back in time and did it all over again?" He illustrated the concept by standing two fingers of one hand, tip-down onto the palm of the other, walking them forward, jumping them backward, and off, then walking them forward on the palm again.

The Iraqi stared at Bent's little finger show, then back at Bent's even, attentive face. I could see the man's brain spinning, even through all the dirt, sweat, bruises, scrapes, and whatever other shit there was between his stubbly chin and dirty hair.

Hell, even my brain was spinning. Was this some weird mind game Bent was playing at here? Inviting fantastical thinking? Maybe give the prisoner's already-abused mind an exit strategy or illusion of power?

"Yes," the Iraqi said.

Ooookay. So what was Bent going to do with that?

"What was different the last time you were here?" Bent asked.

The Iraqi's gaze flicked around the room. "The table did not fall over. You called each other by names."

"What names?"

"You were 'Doc.' A doctor." The Iraqi looked at me. "He is Gordon." At the door. "The guard is Specialist Devers."

"The guard, Specialist Devers, told you this, didn't he?"

The Iraqi shook his head. "The guards only tell us who we are, not who they are."

I thought that sounded about right. Bent looked like he agreed. It didn't explain how the Iraqi knew our names.

Bent walked back to the back of the room and stepped around the overturned small table, avoiding the spilled water, rags, plastic cups, and overturned water jug. He picked up the fallen clipboard and pen, then the chair, and brought them all back to the middle of the room. There he set down the chair directly in front of the kneeling prisoner, sat, and crossed one leg over the other as he lifted the clipboard to his lap, pen at the ready.

"Salim," he said like he might have been conducting a therapy session back in the States, "you said I told you to say 'Mary had a little lamb. Its fleece was white as snow.'"

The Iraqi nodded his head. I noted his body had started to shake. Could have been hunger or fear, but my best guess was muscle fatigue. He'd been in the same awkward kneed since before I'd arrived, with his hands cuffed behind. Probably took a lot of micro-balancing muscles to keep him from falling over as he raised and lowered his head to follow everything that was going on.

"Do you know why I told you to say this?" asked Bent.

The Iraqi shook his head. "No, sir."

"I didn't say."

"No, sir."

"What was happening at the time?"

The Iraqi trembled visibly and shot a glance over at me. "Gordon was getting angry."

"At you?"

"Yes."

I started to interrupt, but Bent held up a hand at me that told me to shut up. So I did, but I felt my internal thermostat rising. I'd been pissed, I realized, from the time I found out my first Comsee assignment was going to be interrogating Iraqis in a prison. Got even more pissed when I started hearing stories about what had been going on at this prison, Abu Ghraib. Even more when I found we were staying in a crumbling cement room that reeked of evil smells. And finally, royally pissed when I'd been called out to my first Tier1 interrogation at 4-fucking-a.m., only to confront Bent, a smirking guard, an already-beaten-up prisoner, and the loss of my personal authority the minute the prisoner spewed out an old English nursery rhyme.

"What did he do?" Bent asked, shooting his own glance my way.

"He slapped my face. He grabbed my wrists and lifted. I had to stand."

"With your wrists behind you?"

"Yes. I screamed."

"I'm not surprised. What did Gordon do then?"

Another glance in my direction, and I could see the prisoner's chest going in and out, great sucking breaths, the motherfucker, like he was terrified. Of *me!*

"You told me to say the words," the prisoner muttered.

"And what did Gordon do?"

"He lifted..." He tried to raise his wrists behind him to demonstrate, and I could *feel* myself wanting to grab them and do what I knew he was about to say I'd done. "Fast! Snap!"

There was silence. The Iraqi was breathing hard. I was breathing hard. Bent was totally still, focused.

"Then?" Bent asked at last.

"I woke up in my cell. Before this. A girl screamed over and over."

Bent nodded. "One last question, Salim. Did you *try* to travel back in time? Did you *think* it? Did you *do* something to make it happen?"

The Iraqi tilted his filthy face to one side like he did not understand the question. What a surprise! The good doc has just asked you if you consciously did magic. And your answer is....

"I did not. I do not know how it works."

"Done it before?" asked Bent.

"Yes. From here. This day, also. When Gordon knocked my head into the floor."

My mouth dropped open. "He's lying. Or delusional. Do you know how many times I've questioned Iraqi detainees? Not once did I ever—"

"Gordon."

Bent said it evenly, but it felt like the kind of slap I'd supposedly given this prisoner in what? Another reality? Why was he even listening to this horse pucky? Worse, he was now getting up from his chair and signaling me to join him in the far corner, out of earshot of the prisoner.

I swallowed a sour taste and wiped my forehead, surprised by how hot I'd become and the sweat beading there. Had to be the desert heat again. I'd forgotten. Even in late October, before five in the morning? Well, no, but....

I walked over and joined Bent as he was halfway to the wall. And I wondered again, like I had on the Hercules flying over here with him, whether maybe some small part of me *was* gay. Because the effect of standing right beside the man, in feeling his body heat, his height and presence, was enough to make me stumble like I couldn't remember how to walk properly. Not *attraction*, though. More like...terror? Serious intimidation, at least. Which was totally reasonable. He was CIA, and Comsee personnel were explicitly outranked by the CIA. He was also a psychiatrist, which meant how many years of post-secondary education? Twelve? Thirteen? I got into the Army straight out of high school. And the buzz I heard on the plane was Bent wasn't just a psychiatrist, he was some kind of crazy genius. It was why the CIA had scooped him. So...yeah. Logical intimidation. That's all it was.

Bent touched my shoulder and leaned in to murmur almost intimately into my ear. "'Mary had a little lamb. Its fleece was white as snow,' was a phrase I would sometimes give to patients whom I was taking through a past-life regression process. There is, of course, insufficient evidence that a patient can actually experience a time when they existed in another body, but there have been enough experiments I can't speak about that support telepathy, hint at body transfer, and suggest consciousness as a force that can exist outside traditional physical structures when given the proper push. In my past-life regression experiments, I hoped to plant a phrase in one person's consciousness that would surface in another's."

Or something like that. He actually used words I'd never heard before and talked about twice as long and really fast. But that bit about consciousness not being locked into one body? I'm pretty sure I got that right. It was a lot like the crazy shit a yoga teacher I used to date would say.

And crazy shit is fine. The yoga babe was hot, so I allowed it. Bent is supposedly brilliant, so whatever. This next part, though, is where my heart just sank down into my gut. These words I do remember clearly. And I'm journaling them as much for CYA as anything. Because, shit....

"Gordon Trench," Bent said in my ear, even closer than before, so I could feel his hot breath. "The US Government hired your boss to send you here to help in the war against terror, correct?"

"Yes," I whispered to the air.

"And you know the articles on torture are suspended for the duration of our duties here, correct?"

"Yes."

"So if I tell you that the very best way to defend our country and its people is to sacrifice the bodily integrity of this Salim Noor al-Rashid, who, his file states, is a thief and terrorist, are you prepared to do it?"

"Is...is that an order?" I felt about two feet tall whispering that. Because, while I knew the CIA outranked me, they didn't exactly have command authority over me. The way my Comsee orders put it was that the CIA could stop or redirect our actions, but they couldn't actually dictate what we *did.*

I thought I felt Bent's lips smile against my ear, and his voice said he knew exactly what I'd just thought. But he said, "Yes, it's an order, Gordon. Here's what I suggest you do..."

5

October 23, 2003 – D

SALIM

"AHHHHHH!"

I think that was my scream as I jerked into consciousness on the floor of my dark cell, kicking and twisting, naked, on the cement. I did not know who I was or where I was for a moment.

Then the sounds of a girl screaming began, and I remembered everything.

So now I lie here in the dark. The twisting about on the sticky cement has reopened some of my wounds because I can slide more easily on the wetness. It is a hollow knowledge because I realize I no longer feel my body.

My skin, I cannot feel.

My limbs, I cannot feel.

I look at my hands, and the fingers I saw Gordon snap in two are whole. I can move them as I always have, though I do not feel them now.

I look down and see no broken ribs, though Gordon kicked some of them in. I can breathe normally, though I do not feel my breath.

My mind has loosened its connection to my body, I think to protect me from feeling the pain I would have felt when Gordon attacked me. I have become unglued in more ways than one—from Time and from my naf, my very self.

Yet the screams of the girl? I am totally consumed by those. They drive me to my feet so I can once again call out in Arabic for the monster Benny to stop. Just STOP!

When they do, I praise Allah.

Then I drop like a collapsed doll to my knees, facing what I think is the direction of Mecca, and use all the power of self-moving that remains in me to say a salawat, asking Allah to send blessings on the Prophet and his family. Then I call on Allah using all his beautiful names. I cup my hands before my naked chest to make dua. Finally, I recite Tasbeeh e Janab e Fatima—many prayers, said many times—until my body can support my voice no longer and I fall forward, smacking my face on the concrete.

I lie still.

Unglued.

Yet, though I am stuck in this time and place, beaten and thrown backward again and again, I will endure. In Allah's name, I will endure my morning with rapist Benny and cruel Specialist Devers, then the different, more extreme cruelties of "Doc" and Gordon.

I will endure them and repeat them as often as I must. For I know Allah will answer my dua in some way, as the prophets say. Trust in Allah.

Allahu Akbar.

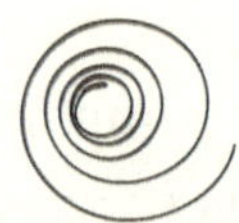

GORDON

Jesus, I don't even want to journal about today. It was too strange and too sick.

But I guess just a short note for when I look back and have adjusted enough to laugh over how easy it was to freak me out. Or maybe it'll be the only record they find that explains why I went bugfuck crazy, and they had to lock me up or put me down.

Anyway, the short version:

First day in the Hard Site, Tier1, started at 4-fucking-a.m. I showed up at the interrogation room and found Dr. Uwe Bent waiting for me, along with a battered, filthy Iraqi prisoner who'd been brought in for theft and terrorism. His name, I learned, was Salim Noor al-Rashid, which, translated from Arabic means something like the healthy, divine light, son of the wise. So this dude was *not* living up to his name.

He had a guard. I got rid of the guard. And suddenly this Iraqi terrorist starts reciting nursery rhymes. First *Mary had a little lamb*, then *Mary, Mary, quite contrary*, then *Peter Pepper.* And every time he did, Dr. Bent went a little more apeshit, pushed me away from the prisoner, and squatted down in front of him to ask him where he'd heard these things.

Then Bent got a scary gleam in his eye and grabbed the prisoner's bruised head with both hands, pulled it closer like he wanted to eat the prisoner's ear, and whispered a whole bunch of somethings to him.

"Personal secrets!" Bent said when he let go of the man's head and straightened up. "No one knows these things now but myself and Salim. And in the next version of this day,"—*Holy shit!*—"if Salim can repeat these things back to me, it will mean for sure that Salim can time travel. And if he can, I am going to take him back to America to study him!"

Take *that*, Donald Rumsfeld!

Oh, and did I mention? Bent also concluded during this intense, long session, that the only way Salim can travel back in time is when he's essentially scared out of his body, or just put through so much agony he (His mind? His soul?) just has to go.

And, of course, I have to be the one doing the scaring and agony infliction, because it Bent did it, it would hurt the long-term therapeutic relationship he had with Salim.

Fuck.

So I kicked, punched, broke parts of the little haji, made him bleed. And at the end of it all, we just had a further brutalized, broken, glassy-eyed wreck who had to be rushed to the infirmary so he didn't actually die.

The guard, Devers, when we got him to open the door, and he saw what I'd done, looked at me like I was *amazing*.

I came back here and puked in my personal toilet.

Oh, Jesus, I am going to Hell.

6

October 23, 2003 – E

SALIM

When Specialist Devers enters my cell to kick me, I get up before he can. I know my body sports all the injuries from the guards last night and my rough sleep, but nothing from Gordon. The injuries he inflicts vanish each time I begin this day again.

And because I am unglued, even yesterday's injuries are nothing. I have no pains, no fears, no desires, no hopes, no plans....

No, that is wrong. I have one plan now.

A small plan.

Sagheer.

Tiny.

If I fail, I will probably die. But this would not be a bad thing.

Specialist Devers grins as he flashes his bright light into my eyes, off and on. "Ha! Yer awful twitchy, sand nigger."

"Do you think so?"

My voice, quietly speaking English, shocks him for a moment.

This is all I need.

I rush at his waist like I have seen American TV linebackers do against quarterbacks. But I do not tackle him. I grab at the metal handcuffs that dangle from the front pocket of his pants.

I succeed but stumble and fall. This maybe saves me from how hard Specialist Devers' flashlight hits me as I go down.

I do not roll like American action heroes. I thud like a bag of fleshy bones. If I could feel more, it would probably hurt. Instead, I scramble to my feet before Specialist Devers reaches me, and I meet his rush with a swinging metal handcuff.

This weapon hits him on the cheek, knocking his head to the side so he staggers, bleeding.

He does not fall but blindly steps past me like I am not there.

I spin and leap after him, cracking my metal handcuffs into his skull, his neck, his back, until he crumples to the ground with me on top of him, silently thudding my cuffs into him over and over until the metal splashes in a mess of blood and bone, the man's naf now gone.

I stop.

The only sound is my heavy breathing.

This dead man is separate from me.

My bloody hands and arms and shirt and face separate from me.

A voice I recognize as belonging to the man in the cell beside me calls out to me low and questioning. I do not hear what he is asking because he is separate from me as well.

I am unglued.

...

When I finally take something in, it is Benny, speaking Arabic to me in hushed, frightened tones. I turn and look at him. The blood of my vanquished torturer drips from my entire body, and I see the power of that in Benny's eyes. His terror and awe.

"I can get you to America," I whisper in Arabic.

Benny blinks at me. If he is surprised I read his deepest yearning, he does not show it. He simply nods and asks in our language, "How?"

I explain it to him. Although he finds it hard to believe, my manner and what I did with the handcuffs convince him I am telling the truth as I know it.

I whisper the plan to him a second and third time while I am using the shirt I have torn off Specialist Devers to clean my body as best I can. Benny offers me a water bottle he carries, and I use it to clean my face and the handcuffs. I drink the rest.

Benny has stripped out of his clothing and handed it to me. As I dress, he rolls about on the floor and, almost comically, bangs his head and naked body into the rough spots to create bruises and scrapes. I make him scoop blood from Specialist Devers' corpse and work it into the grime he has accumulated, especially in his hair. Then he drags Devers' body to the furthest back shadows of the cell, stripped, darkened with grime, and face down. I ask him to pull the foul hood and his prison keys from wherever Devers carried them.

When Benny comes back, I am dressed, and he is the naked prisoner, much my size, weight, age, and general appearance. Only Americans who know us well could tell we have changed.

I take the hood and keys from him and whisper the plan to him one last time.

And because Benny is more focused, motivated, and smarter than I am, he listens closely. When I am done, he whispers the plan back to me, first in Arabic, then in English. He knows the tunes to "Mary Had a Little Lamb" and the other nonsense rhymes the doctor gave me to grab his attention each time I met him. I did not know they were songs.

He repeats the secret stories the doctor told me. One is about the dog of the doctor's childhood friend. When he and the friend were in fifth grade, the doctor stole this dog and experimented on it until it died. No one found out.

A second story is about seeing a professor in medical school rape the dean's wife. The doctor saw this because he was in the wife's closet. He was a student at the time but had been having relations with this woman as well.

"Are these stories true?" Benny whispers in Arabic when he is done.

"I do not know. It does not matter. The doctor will say they were just made up, but if you say them, he will believe you can travel back in time because how else could you know?"

"And then he will take me to America?"

"He said he will. You will be his great discovery."

"I will be rich! I will have a big apartment, many girlfriends. I will drive a Mercedes-Benz."

"If Allah wills." Then the haram of lying by omission compels me to tell him, in full detail, what the doctor made Gordon do so that I would time travel.

"Because of this place!" Benny said. "Because here it is normal. Not in America! In America there are laws!"

I stare at him. Does he not understand the doctor's story of the dog?

"Let's go!" he says.

I hesitate one moment more, then handcuff Benny's hands behind his back. I stuff the foul-smelling hood into one of the many pockets of my new American battle dress. Then, quietly, with Devers' keys in a different pocket, I walk this very naked, vulnerable Benny quietly out the door and down the hallway.

It is dark, and most of the prisoners are asleep, but one who is not, calls out softly, "Insallah." *If Allah wills.*

I nod at the dark shape behind the bars and keep walking.

Benny directs me through a door to the right, down a short hall, and stops. "This is it," he whispers in Arabic.

I nod and pull out the hood.

Benny sees it, and his eyes can't help but widen in fear. "A moment," he says.

I wait.

"I drove here in a car. A yellow Volkswagen Golf hatchback. One of the headlights is missing. It has my helmet and body armor. On loan. It is parked in the lot just outside the center block." He gave me directions. "The keys and my identification card are in your right breast pocket." He gestures with his chin. "Make sure you drive south to get out. That's the only exit."

I reach into the pocket and find the keys and keycard. I probably would have noticed the weight if I had any feeling in my body. "Thank you."

He forces a grin. "You give me your identity. I give you mine."

I nod. He closes his eyes. I pull the hood over his head and bang on the door. Then I open it.

Inside, I see that Gordon has already arrived. He looks angry as always. The doctor is seated in his usual place against the back wall, over to one side, almost hiding behind a table with glasses, a mug, rags, and a clipboard.

Both men look surprised to see an Iraqi man ushering in the prisoner.

"I'm a translator, visiting Specialist Devers. He had to use the toilet. Bad food." I made the gesture over my stomach of food churning.

"You going to translate then?" asks Gordon.

"No need. He speaks English."

Gordon and the doctor exchange looks and I realize I did this wrong. What Iraqi translator would refuse a request to be of service? Their livelihood is built on being helpful to all Americans.

If I could feel anything, I think my body would tremble or sweat now. They would catch me for sure. As it is, I remain cool, and the two Americans aren't sure.

Gordon walks toward me. "Why's your face all cut up and bruised like that?"

"A car bomb," I lie. It is haram, a sin. But I think the part of me that loves Allah, that is gripped by feelings of worship and guilt, love and loss, pain and joy—this part is something I have also lost in my ungluing. All I do now is survive.

"You said you're only visiting here. Who're you normally translating for?"

"Corporal Lark, Third Infantry," I said, the lie popping out randomly from a conversation I heard between the guards.

I realize then that neither American knows anything about who is fighting here in Baghdad. Gordon looks blank. The doctor has already forgotten my face and turned away.

Before I can escape, however, Gordon grabs my arm.

"Show me some ID," he says.

I answer by yanking off Benny's hood and kicking him casually behind his knees. "Kneel!"

Benny does. I stare fiercely at him, but Gordon has not left us.

"Your *ID*," Gordon says again, voice hard.

So Benny decides to sing. "*Mary had a little lamb, little lamb, lit-tle lamb! Mary had a little lamb. Its fleece was white as snow!*"

The doctor shoots up from his seat, knocking over the table just as he did the last two times.

"What the—?" Gordon spins to face him. Then spins back to Benny as the kneeling naked man breaks into a chant of *Mary, Mary, Quite Contrary.*

The doctor has hurried over to face Benny, physically pushing Gordon away from him and from me. For just a moment, he aims his sparkling blue eyes at me. They show no recognition of ever having met me as he says, "Leave, translator. Go find a car bomb or something."

I nod, turn, and leave, closing the heavy steel door behind me.

A few minutes later, I am in the parking lot outside the Hard Site, my eyes searching the pre-dawn darkness for a VW hatchback that might be yellow in the sunshine. After three failed attempts, I find a car that takes Benny's key and climb into the driver's seat. As I start the engine, I fear I might have forgotten how to drive since I have not driven since my father died.

I pull forward smoothly, praise Allah.

Unfortunately, I cannot tell north from south. I do not read stars, and there is not yet a glimmer of dawn for direction.

Muttering a dua under my breath, I rummage through the back seat and find Benny's borrowed American helmet. I put it on the seat beside me. Then I turn on the car headlights, choose one of the four roads leading out of the lot, and drive.

As I clear the edge of the Hard Site, an explosion outside the prison walls lights the outline of the exit gate. I squeal right, thumping across sandy scrub, find the road again, slow down, and take the next left cautiously. When I stop at the gate, the half-asleep guard glances up, says, "See ya, Benny," and waves me through.

WHAT FOLLOWS IS THREE hours of searching road signs, close calls with American patrols, and driving—Thank you, Benny, for leaving me a wallet filled with cash!—before I approach the small farming town of Aldor on the Tigris River, 150 miles north of Baghdad.

Before I reach it, I turn down a dusty road at random and park outside an old stone farmhouse. I see no one, but smoke curls out of the chimney. An Iraqi welcome.

Why am I here?

I am dead inside. Unglued from my body. My naf is a wandering, lost thing.

Then I remember how, during the drive here, the sun began to rise far in the east, and I felt a flickering urge to slide into its warmth like I once immersed myself in everything.

My hand grasps the handle of the car door.

I think...I must be a child again. Learn what it is to feel, smell, taste, hear, laugh, cry, love, and praise Allah.

And when I grow up just a little bit, I will seek out Nazyah and, like my country, try to live again.

I open the door and step out of the car.

Epilogue: April 28, 2004

GORDON

OKAY, GORDO. YOU DON'T know if you're saved or damned? Write it out. Record what happened.

The key moment, I think, was when I finally turned off the *60 Minutes II* report on CBS about Abu Ghraib. I was sickened all over again by the reality of that much depravity among our own troops, once-good American boys and girls.

And the report didn't even *mention* the brutal killing of Specialist Devers, found the same day Dr. Uwe Bent took a fast plane out of there with prisoner Salim Noor al-Rashid in his personal custody. Didn't mention the search for Bakri AKA Benny Faiz, either. He was probably Devers' killer. Also known to have raped a bunch of women and girls in the Tier2 of the Hard Site.

And me? If I hadn't taken my cue from Dr. Bent and left the same day, I would have been caught in all of it. Somehow. Because *the idiots took* PHOTOGRAPHS *of everything! How stupid could you be?* And I would have committed abuses. Torture. Something. I don't know how I'm certain of it, but I am. That place, that country, the politics—they got under my skin. But I already had a rage there. I wanted to hurt people, brown people, who were attacking America!

I think that's why Comsee sent me. And why they let me return when I came to my senses. And later gave me a handsome retirement package after working for them less than a year. They were already deep into the Abu Ghraib clusterfuck. Couldn't afford any more whistleblowers.

But where did that leave me now?

I jumped up from my couch in my lousy little apartment in downtown Minneapolis and paced my worn carpet. I'd come back here more out of habit than anything. My old friends? My family? What could I tell them about what I'd been doing for the past year? How could *I* even live with what I'd been prepared to do? It all—

The phone rang.

Body trembling with a strange premonition, I walked over to my kitchen and picked my handset off its wall cradle. "Yeah?"

"Gordon, this is Uwe Bent. You remember me?"

Something went straight from the pit of my stomach up to my throat. I swallow hard to push it back down and knotted my fingers into the curls of the phone cord. "Sure, Doc. What can I do for you?"

"Actually, I think it might be more what I can do for you. You've been watching CBS, I assume."

Another rise of sick as my eyes darted to the black TV screen. "Yeah."

"I've heard...stories of things you did for me that you will not even be aware of."

Swallowed it back down. "Like what?"

"Necessary things. Things that let Salim free himself from his body and jump back to an earlier one."

"Oh, God. You mean I tortured him."

"More or less."

"And he time traveled. Or his mind did." *Tell me you're bullshitting me. Tell me!*

"He did."

"You're con*vinced*." Jesus, I wished *I* could leave my body. Leave this reality. One where I knew I'd done exactly what I'd run to get away from, to *prevent* myself from doing.

"Convinced enough that I have persuaded the CIA to let me form a semi-autonomous department within it to find more people like Salim and study them. I want you to be a part of this."

"Because I do...necessary things."

"Yes."

Yeah. There it was. A sudden flood, not of vomit or disgust, but excitement. It was so intense it made me want to yell, *Hell, YES! Sign me up!*

But the simultaneous, smaller flood of fear over what I would become made me say, "Let me think on it." I started to hang up. "Wait. What's it called? Your new group?"

I could almost hear Bent smile on the other end of the line. "I don't think the name will mean much to you until you understand what we're doing. Just know that it will go beyond simply locating and studying time travelers. It will change who runs the world and what they make of it."

I could feel his words resonate inside me, vibrating against both my excitement and my shame, tearing me apart. "Just give me the fucking name."

"SCATTER."

I took a breath as it settled into me, drawing together all the crazy I'd been through, thought I'd fled from, found I hadn't at all, and desperately desired.

Bent's voice almost purred as he said, "Well, Gordon?"

I swallowed, nodded, and flipped my finger at the TV screen, the town, the whole messed-up world that needed a good shake-up.

"I'm in," I said.

Afterword

I hope you enjoyed *Unglued: The First Time Traveler.* If you found it engaging, please leave a review at www.goodreads.com and/or wherever you bought it.

And if you'd like to dive into the series itself, ask for the books below at your local bookstore or buy from your favorite online bookstore.

Jackson is haunted by his turbulent past. When an attempted kidnapping leaves him with unexpected powers, can he use them to unlock the truth of what really happened?

He swore off time travel to re-build his mental health, but Jackson has finally found out who took his brother. Playing it safe is no longer an option.

Jackson surrendered himself to protect the people he loves. Now he's in a fight to hang onto his sanity, his brother, and the future of humanity.

About the Author

Terry Hayman is a former lawyer who grew up in a military family with a father who was a general and a mother who was a psychologist. He's the author of many novels and over a hundred short stories under various names. You can learn more about his work and sign up for his newsletter, at www.terryhayman.com.

Also by Terry Hayman

NOVELS & NOVELLAS
Jumpback
SCATTER
Fuse
Chasing the Minotaur
Jessica Falls
Shelter
Bone Dance
Raised by a Vampire

SHORT STORY COLLECTIONS
Being Human: 5 heartfelt tales of fantasy and science fiction set on earth
Off-World: 5 tales of adventure set on other planets
Dark Paths: 5 short stories exploring the darker sides of human nature
Life Knots: 5 stories of ordinary people fighting their destinies
Messed Up: 5 stories of crime and consequences
Used by Magic: 5 stories of people caught up by powers unseen
Shorties: A collection of sublimely quick story punches to the head, heart, and gut
Vamp: 5 stories of bloodsuckers, romantic and otherwise